Feisty Fannie Fishwitch

Hops on her broom and flies

Toward the western skies

Fannie Fishwitch is far from gloom

She has her special broom

It takes her to California-----a very big state

And what a fate

She flies under the world famous Golden Gate

She meets up with her school of fish friends

Jumps off her broom without a fuss

And hops on the School of Fish Bus

Her fishy friends are so glad

To have Fannie aboard

They won't be sad

Fannie Fishwitch lifts any fish out of gloom

With her very special happy broom!

HAPPY HALLEBOOIA!

July 2018

Steer your broom
A way from gloom!
Christine Okezie
aka Fish Wish Chris